6-2-93 (Jarrin 9 on)

W9-BFQ-270

3 1593 000 39988 8

8·17·23 8 Vouts 6/23

very Damaged

I am an Aro Publishing Twenty Word Book

My twenty words are:

Waldo	for
little	him
feet	with
big	can
beak	cannot
likes	fast
to	last
swim	surprise
is	and
hard	flies

ISBN 0-89868-157-X — Library Bound
ISBN 0-89868-158-8 — Soft Bound

FUNNY FARM BOOKS

Waldo Duck

Story by Wendy Kanno
Pictures by Bob Reese

 ARO PUBLISHING

Waldo's

little feet.

Waldo's big beak.

Waldo likes to swim.

Swimming is hard for him,

With Waldo's

little feet.

With Waldo's

little feet.

Waldo's big surprise,

Waldo swims and flies,

With Waldo's big beak.

Waldo can swim fast.

Cannot come in last,

With Waldo's big beak.